DISCARDED

P9-BYN-538

John Simatovich Elem.

Brimhall
turns to
MAGIC

by Judy Delton

illustrated by Bruce Degen

Lothrop, Lee & Shepard Company
A DIVISION OF WILLIAM MORROW & CO., INC.
NEW YORK

To Elaine Knox-Wagner, whose magic touches
what I write and who I am.

Text copyright © 1979 by Judy Delton
Illustrations copyright © 1979 by Bruce Degen
All rights reserved. No part of this book may be
reproduced or utilized in any form or by any means,
electronic or mechanical, including photocopying,
recording or by any information storage and retrieval
system, without permission in writing from the
Publisher. Inquiries should be addressed to Lothrop,
Lee & Shepard Company, 105 Madison Ave., New
York, N. Y. 10016.
Printed in the United States of America.
First Edition

1 2 3 4 5 6 7 8 9 10

Library of Congress Cataloging in Publication Data
Delton, Judy.
   Brimhall turns to magic.
   (A Fun-To-Read book)
   SUMMARY: Brimhall learns enough magic to make
a rabbit appear in a hat, but not enough to make him
vanish.
   [1. Magic tricks—Fiction. 2. Animals—Fiction. 3.
Friendship—Fiction] I. Degen, Bruce. II. Title.
PZ7.D388Bu   [E]   78-12141
ISBN 0-688-41878-3   ISBN 0-688-51878-8 lib. bdg.

CONTENTS

1 Brimhall's New Class · 5

2 Magic Made Easy? · 8

3 Brimhall Tries Again · 23

4 Bear Takes Charge · 34

5 The Farewell Dinner · 43

6 Still More Magic · 55

1

BRIMHALL'S NEW CLASS

"Bear!" called Brimhall,

throwing open the front door.

Bear looked up from his book.

"Brimhall, are you home from

your painting class already?"

he said.

"The art class was filled, Bear.

They had no room for new students.

I signed up for a better class.

It's called 'Magic Made Easy'!"

"Why, Brimhall, that sounds
exciting!" said Bear.
Brimhall whipped out a deck of
cards. "Pick a card, any card,
Bear."
Bear rubbed his paws together
and drew a card.

Brimhall shuffled the rest.
Then he looked carefully through
the deck. "The card you are
holding is a... an ace of spades!"
Bear looked at his card. "Well,
you're close, Brimhall. I have
the queen of hearts."
Brimhall frowned.
"You've only had one lesson,
Brimhall," said Bear kindly.
"These things take time."
The two cousins turned out the
light and got ready for bed.

2

MAGIC MADE EASY?

The next day Brimhall practiced
his card tricks some more.
All week he read his magic book
and tried new tricks.
After the second lesson, Brimhall
came home very excited.
He was carrying a big black bag.
"Bear!" he cried. "Wait until
you see this! I have something
exciting to show you!"

Bear took off his apron. "Wait,
Brimhall. Let me call Raccoon
and Porcupine over, so they can
see it, too." Bear rushed to
the phone. "Come as soon as you
can," he said. "Brimhall is now
a magician, you know. He has
learned a fine new trick. You
will be the first to see it!"

While they waited for their
guests, Bear and Brimhall set
three chairs in a row. They put
Bear's table up in front.
Raccoon and Porcupine rushed
in, all out of breath.
"We're ready, Brimhall," said Bear.

Brimhall opened his bag
and took out a large black hat.
"You see this hat?" he asked.
The audience nodded. "Yes! Yes!"
they said.

Brimhall held up the hat.
"Look inside the hat," he said.
The audience looked inside.
"There is nothing inside this
hat," Brimhall declared.
The audience agreed.

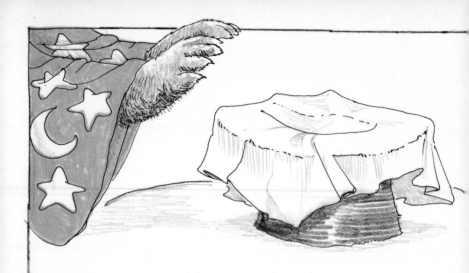

Brimhall put the hat down on
the table. "Now I will place
this large white handkerchief
over the hat," said Brimhall.
The audience watched closely.
"Now there must be absolute
silence," Brimhall said.
No one moved a muscle.
Brimhall closed his eyes and
held his paws over the hat.

"Abra-cadabra

Kalamazoo

Here is a large

White rabbit for you!"

Brimhall opened his eyes and stuck
a paw into the hat. He pulled out
a large white rabbit.

Bear shouted and clapped. "You
are so clever, Brimhall! A
rabbit! From an empty hat!"
"That is amazing!" cried Raccoon.
"That is MAGIC!" said Porcupine.
The audience clapped and clapped.
Brimhall and the rabbit bowed.

"Now then," said Brimhall, "I
will make the rabbit disappear!"
Brimhall picked the rabbit
up, put him back in the hat,
and covered him with the
handkerchief.

> *"Abra-cadabra*
>
> *Kalamazoo.*
>
> *Make this rabbit*
>
> *Vanish from view!"*

Brimhall opened his eyes.
The rabbit was still in the hat.
The audience could see his white
ears sticking out the top.

"I must have made a little
mistake," said Brimhall. "I
will try again." Brimhall held
his paws over the hat. He closed
his eyes and thought hard.

"Abra-cadabra

Ginger root beer

Now may this rabbit

At once disappear!"

Brimhall opened his eyes.
The rabbit was still in the hat.

The rabbit stretched. He yawned.

The audience waited politely.

Brimhall walked around the hat.

He looked under the table and up

at the ceiling. "Ah," he said.

"I believe I know what the

problem is."

"Good," said the rabbit, pulling

his ears into the hat.

Bear and Porcupine and Raccoon

crossed their paws for luck.

"Abra-cadabra

Ziz boom bam

Disappear, Rabbit—

I tell you to scram!"

"I've had enough," said the

rabbit, climbing out of the hat.

"My legs are stiff."

Brimhall got out his magic book.

The rabbit came over to Porcupine

and Raccoon. "My name is Roger,"

he said, shaking their paws. "I

don't usually have time between

magic acts to meet anyone. But

with *this* magician"—Roger looked

at Brimhall—"I may be here a while."

"I will make you a bed on the
sofa, Roger," said Bear.
Brimhall was still reading.

"Well, we had better be going,"
said Raccoon and Porcupine. "Thank
you for the magic show, Brimhall."
Brimhall was muttering magic
words to himself.

"Brimhall," said Bear, "don't
feel so bad. You did pull a
rabbit out of a hat. I don't
know anyone who can do that."

"Still," said Brimhall, "a rabbit
that you pull out of a hat is
SUPPOSED to disappear. I must
be saying the wrong magic words."
Brimhall shut his book. "I will
try again tomorrow."

"I say," said Roger, "can you
lend me some pajamas? I don't
happen to have mine with me."
"Dear me," said Bear. "I don't
believe I have anything to fit
you. Brimhall, do you have
anything to fit Roger?"

"I have a large muffler," said
Brimhall. "It should be just right."
Roger wrapped himself in
Brimhall's muffler and lay down
on the sofa.
Soon all three animals were
sound asleep.

3

BRIMHALL TRIES AGAIN

The next morning Roger was up
early.

He made toast and a pot of tea
and called Bear and Brimhall.

"Why, what a nice surprise,
Roger," said Bear.

"Yes," said Brimhall. "A cup of
tea wakes me up so I am ready to
work. I'll be off to the library
now."

Bear and Roger sat down to visit.
"You have a fine home here,"
said Roger.

"Thank you," said Bear. "I am
sure by tonight you will be
back in your own home."

"Oh, I have never had a home,"
said Roger. "I am always on the
road. But I do like show business."

"What an exciting life you must
have!" said Bear, getting out the
vegetables for stew.

"Carrots!" said Roger. "I will
peel them for you, Bear."
"Why, thank you, Roger. That
will be a big help."
Roger and Bear talked as they
worked. Soon the stew was on
the stove.

Brimhall came in whistling.
"I have it," he said. "A new,
more up-to-date magic book."
He put the black hat on the
table. "All right, Roger. You
can get in the hat."
"Dear me," said Bear. "Can't it
wait until we have our lunch?
I am sure Roger would like a
dish of stew before he leaves."
"Fine, fine," said Brimhall.

After lunch, Roger helped wash
the dishes. "Well," he said at
last, "I guess this is good-bye."
Roger shook Bear's paw and
Brimhall's. "Thank you for
everything," he said.
He climbed into the hat.
Brimhall covered the hat with
the handkerchief. He held out
his paws and closed his eyes.
He said the new magic words
from the library book.
Bear waved good-bye to Roger.

Brimhall opened his eyes.

He looked in the hat.

Then he frowned.

"He's still here," said Brimhall.

Roger climbed out of the hat.

"Let me see that book," he said.

"Maybe you can stay one more night,"
said Brimhall. "Can't he, Bear?"

"Why—yes—another night would
be fine, I suppose," said Bear,
who was mixing an angel cake.

"This is a problem," said Roger. "I really should have my own pajamas. The muffler is a bit scratchy."

"It will only be until tomorrow," said Brimhall cheerfully. "Do you know how to play chess, Roger?"

"No, but I play checkers. Do you play checkers, Brimhall?"

"No, but Bear and I would love to learn, wouldn't we, Bear?"

When the cake was in the oven, Roger taught Bear and Brimhall how to play checkers. After that, Roger tap-danced for them.

"Why, you dance very well," said Brimhall. Roger taught Brimhall a few of his dance steps.

"This is fun!" said Brimhall,

dancing across the kitchen floor.

"Bear, come try. It's not hard."

"No, you go ahead, Brimhall. I'll

just look through your magic book

here for a little while..."

Bear turned to the part about

rabbits and hats.

Brimhall and Roger danced and

sang. Then they popped corn and

brought Bear a bowl.

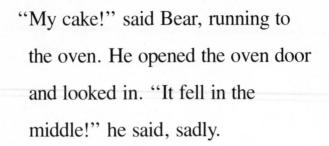

"My cake!" said Bear, running to
the oven. He opened the oven door
and looked in. "It fell in the
middle!" he said, sadly.

"You must have read the recipe
wrong," said Brimhall, dancing
across the floor.

"It is not the recipe," said
Bear, watching the oven shake as
Brimhall danced.

After dinner, Brimhall and Roger
played checkers.

Bear read more of the magic book.

"Well," yawned Roger, "I think
I'll turn in. It's been a real
pleasure, Brimhall. We had a
fine time. Good night, Bear."
Roger wrapped himself in the
muffler and curled up on the sofa.

"Ah, Bear," he said, "would you
mind turning off the light? I
can't get to sleep with it on."
Bear closed his book with
a thud. Then he went into his
room and shut the door.

4

BEAR TAKES CHARGE

The next morning Roger whistled
as he took his shower. "Oh, Bear,"
he called. "Do you have any shampoo?
I came without any, you know."
Bear did not answer. He got his
shampoo out of the cupboard and
gave it to Roger.

"Thank you, Bear," called Roger.
After his shower, Roger brushed
his fur and put on his tie.

Then he called to Bear, "Ah,
Bear, do you have an extra
toothbrush? I came without one,
you know."

"NO," said Bear. "I don't have
an extra toothbrush, Roger. Just
rinse out your mouth—that should
do for today."

When Brimhall got up he made
breakfast for everyone.

Brimhall and Roger sang as they
washed the dishes.

Then they left to go into town.

"We'll be back soon," Brimhall
told Bear.

"Take your time," said Bear,
slamming the door after them.

"This house is too small for
three," he added to himself.

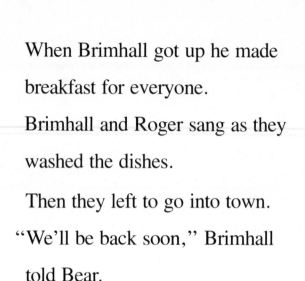

A while later Raccoon and
Porcupine knocked at the door.
"We wondered if you wanted to go
on a picnic with us, Bear," they
said. "And Brimhall, too. Is he
at home?"

"No," said Bear. "Brimhall and
Roger went into town."

"Roger!" said Raccoon. "Is he
still here?"

Just then Brimhall and Roger
came up the path.

"Look at my new silk pajamas!"
said Roger. "Brimhall bought
them for me. And I have a new
red toothbrush and a pair of
warm slippers."

"Just in case," said Brimhall.

Bear took Brimhall aside.

"Brimhall!" Bear whispered. "When is Roger going to leave?"

"Today," said Brimhall. "As soon as we get back from fishing. I thought I would take Roger down to Clover Creek. Imagine, Bear, he has never gone fishing! Why don't you and Raccoon and Porcupine come, too?"

"I think you had better talk to
your magic teacher instead!"
hissed Bear. "And see what you
are doing wrong."
"Plenty of time when we get
back," said Brimhall. "No rush."
Brimhall went to the cellar to
fetch the fishing poles. Then
Brimhall and Roger and Porcupine
and Raccoon left for Clover Creek.
"I will just have to call the
teacher myself," thought Bear,
showing them to the door.
"I will catch a fine fish for supper,
Bear," called Roger, waving.

As soon as they were gone, Bear

went to the phone. He asked to

see the magic teacher that afternoon.

After lunch, Bear set off.

When Bear returned, Brimhall was
counting fish and Roger was
dressed up in his new pajamas.
"I know what we are doing wrong,"
Bear announced. "Tonight, after
dinner, I will perform the trick
that will make Roger disappear."
"Really?" said Brimhall. "I
didn't know you were interested
in magic, Bear."

5

THE FAREWELL DINNER

That night Bear set the table
with his best china.
He put flowers in the center of
the table, and two candles in
silver holders.
"This is a special dinner," said
Bear. "It is Roger's farewell
dinner. I have invited Raccoon
and Porcupine to join us."
Raccoon and Porcupine arrived.

Everyone sat down at the table.
When they were ready to eat,
Roger tapped his spoon on his
water glass. "I would like to say
a few words," he said. "Thank you
for your kindness, Brimhall and
Bear. It has been"—Roger sniffled
—"just like having my own home.
I will never forget such fine
times and fine friends."

Roger hugged each of his friends.

A tear fell from Raccoon's eye.

Porcupine was crying onto his

plate.

Brimhall sniffed loudly.

No one could eat much fish.

Bear cleared his throat. "Let's

get on with it," he said, standing

up. "We'll leave the dishes for

—er—later."

Bear got Brimhall's black hat out of the closet.

"Now," said Bear, "we must cover the hat with a BLACK cloth, not a white one. You can get in the hat, Roger."

Roger climbed into the hat.

Bear covered the hat with a black cloth. He walked around the hat three times and crossed his paws.

"Rabbit, rabbit

By the hair on my toe

Disappear, disappear—

I tell you to GO!"

Bear took the black cloth away.

He looked inside the hat.

"ROGER!" he said. "What are you
doing in there?"

"Maybe you need more lessons,
Bear," said Roger, yawning. "And
now, if no one minds, I will get
ready for bed."

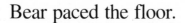

Bear paced the floor.

"Don't feel bad, Bear," Brimhall

said kindly. "It's not as easy

as it looks."

Raccoon thought for a moment. He

whispered to Porcupine. Porcupine

whispered back. "I might be

able to make Roger disappear,"

said Raccoon suddenly. "With

Porcupine's help."

"YOU?" said Bear. "What do you
know about magic?"

"Well," said Raccoon, "my uncle
was part of a magic act."

"Roger!" called Bear.

Roger came out of the bathroom
in his silk pajamas. He had his
toothbrush in his paw.

"It seems Raccoon knows some
magic, Roger," said Bear kindly.

"Get back in the hat."

Roger sighed. He waved his
toothbrush and climbed in the hat.

"The black cloth or the white one?"
he asked Raccoon.

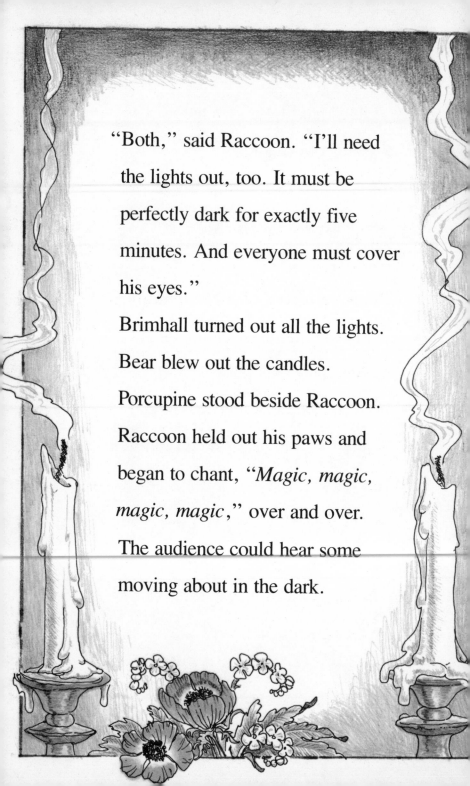

"Both," said Raccoon. "I'll need the lights out, too. It must be perfectly dark for exactly five minutes. And everyone must cover his eyes."

Brimhall turned out all the lights. Bear blew out the candles. Porcupine stood beside Raccoon. Raccoon held out his paws and began to chant, "*Magic, magic, magic, magic*," over and over. The audience could hear some moving about in the dark.

When it was quiet, Raccoon said,
"All right, turn on the lights,
Brimhall."
When the lights went on, Raccoon
was holding up the empty black
hat. A few white rabbit hairs
were clinging to the sides.

"Why!" said Bear. "I do believe
Roger is GONE! You did it,
Raccoon!"

"Where is Porcupine?" asked
Brimhall. "Did you make him
disappear, too?"

Just then Porcupine rushed in
and stood beside Raccoon.

"Well, I've got to hand it to you,
Raccoon," said Bear. "You are
better at magic than we are.
Now, would anyone care for tea?"

"No," said Raccoon. "I think we
should be getting home." He and
Porcupine said good-bye and left.

Brimhall helped Bear wash the
dishes.

"Well, it's back to the chessboard
tonight," Brimhall said.

"Yes," said Bear, "we haven't
played for a long time."

Bear put the dishes away.

He and Brimhall played three
games of chess.

"It's quiet," said Bear, listening
to the clock tick. "I do hope
Roger has a good place to stay.
I should have given him a jar of
his favorite jam to take along."
Brimhall won the third game and
the cousins went to bed.

6

STILL MORE MAGIC

The next morning Bear got up
early. After breakfast, he baked
a carrot and honey cake.
Brimhall went outside to water
his plants.
At noon the two cousins ate lunch
in silence.
"This is Roger's favorite cake,"
Bear said at last. "It's a shame
he can't have a piece."

"I miss his tap-dancing," said
Brimhall. "You know, Bear, I
believe I will give up magic and
sign up for tap-dancing at the
school." Brimhall picked up a
folder. "The first class is tonight."
"I should have sent some cake along
with Roger," said Bear, looking
at the table. "You know, Brimhall,
I never thought I would say this,
but I do miss Roger. I am a bit
sorry he is gone."

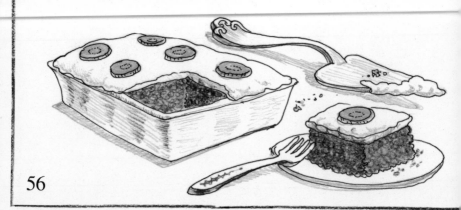

Brimhall looked at the closet
door. He got up and opened it.
He took down the black hat.
"Well—" Brimhall said, swinging
the hat around on one paw.
Just then there was a knock on
the door. In walked Raccoon.
"What are you doing with your
black hat, Brimhall?" he asked.

"Thinking about Roger," said
Brimhall. "We miss him. Perhaps
I'll try the hat trick again.
That's the part I am good at—
pulling rabbits OUT of hats."
"Hold it," said Bear, putting up
a paw. "How do you know we would
get the same rabbit? And what
you are NOT good at is getting
rabbits to leave again."

Raccoon was thinking. "Let me borrow your hat, Brimhall," he said. "Now you and Bear close the curtains and cover your eyes. Think very hard about Roger." Ten minutes later, Raccoon and Porcupine were standing in front of Brimhall and Bear with the black hat. "Open the curtains!" they cried. "Uncover your eyes!"

Out of the hat jumped Roger.

"ROGER!" cried Bear.

"I am just here to visit," Roger
said, hugging Bear and Brimhall.

"I have been at Porcupine's house
since Raccoon made me—ah—
disappear."

"So that's what happened when
Raccoon was a magician!" said
Brimhall. "That is cheating—
Porcupine just took you to his
house!"

"Raccoon made Roger disappear.
That's more than you did,
Brimhall," whispered Bear.

"I am going to rent a home five rabbit holes from here!" said Roger. "I think it's time I settled down."

The five friends had a party to celebrate Roger's return.

Finally, everyone left for home.
Bear gave Roger a jar of carrot
jam to take along.
"It is good to have Roger back,"
said Brimhall, looking at the
clock. "And now I am off to my
dancing class."
Bear hummed as he cleaned up the
party things. He put the black
hat on the shelf in the closet
and closed the door.
Then Bear got ready for bed and
crawled in.

"Roger is nearby," said Bear to
himself as he closed his eyes,
"and Brimhall will be home soon."
Bear felt warm and cozy.
Just before he drifted off to
sleep he heard a crash and some
rumbling and a few notes of music.
"I must be dreaming," said Bear,
and he turned over and fell asleep.

Lothrop *Fun-To-Read* Books

Animal Cracks by Robert Quackenbush

Brimhall Comes to Stay by Judy Delton, pictures by
    Cyndy Szekeres

Brimhall Turns to Magic by Judy Delton, pictures by
    Bruce Degen

Calling Doctor Quack by Robert Quackenbush

Detective Mole by Robert Quackenbush

Detective Mole and the Secret Clues by
Robert Quackenbush

Detective Mole and the Tip-Top Mystery by
    Robert Quackenbush

Jillions of Jerbils by Arnold Dobrin

Mr. Snow Bunting's Secret by Robert Quackenbush

Moose's Store by Robert Quackenbush

The Mouses' Terrible Christmas by True Kelley and
    Steven Lindblom, pictures by True Kelley

Old One-Eye Meets His Match by Roy Doty

Pete Pack Rat by Robert Quackenbush

Pete Pack Rat and the Gila Monster Gang by
    Robert Quackenbush

Sheriff Sally Gopher and the Haunted Dance Hall by
    Robert Quackenbush

Space Hijack! by Nancy Robison, pictures by
    Edward Frascino

Take Me to the Moon! by Sal Murdocca

Tuttle's Shell by Sal Murdocca

UFO Kidnap! by Nancy Robison, pictures by
    Edward Frascino

E DEL   4049
Brimhall turns to magic /

John Simatovich Elementay School